ZIG ZAG

The Cat in the Coat

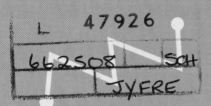
First published 2005
Evans Brothers Limited
2A Portman Mansions
Chiltern St
London W1U 6NR

British Library Cataloguing in Publication Data

French, Vivian
         The cat in the coat. - (Zig zags)
         1. Children's stories - Pictorial works
         I. Title
         823.9'14 [J]

ISBN 0 237 52847 9

Printed in China by WKT Company Limited

Series Editor: Nick Turpin
Design: Robert Walster
Production: Jenny Mulvanny
Series Consultant: Gill Matthews

ZIG ZAG

The Cat in the Coat

by Vivian French

illustrated by Alison Bartlett

Evans

A cat in a coat met
a goat in a hat.

"Mr Goat!" said the cat,
"what a very fine hat!"

"Mr Cat," said the goat,
"that's a very fine coat."

9

"Dear friend," said the cat,
"do ride in my boat."

"Is it safe?" said the goat,
"are you sure it will float?"

13

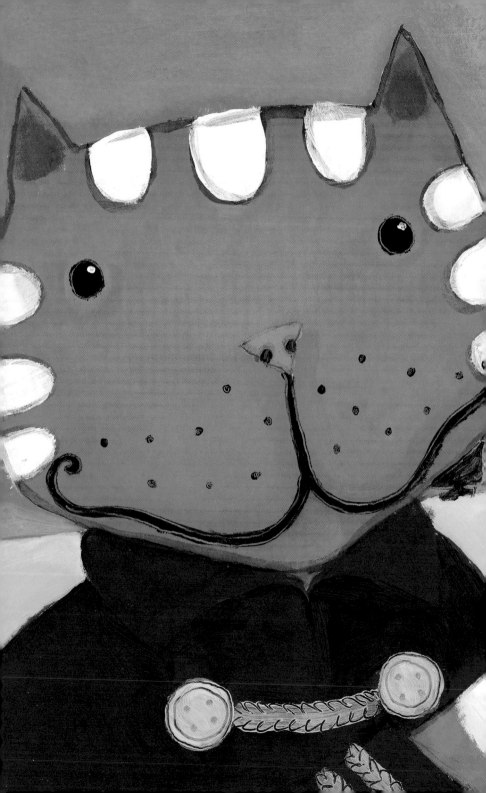

"Oh yes," said the cat,
"my boat is the best."

"So come for a ride –
do please come inside.
Sit down here and rest."

18

The goat made a leap and
he jumped right inside.

"What a very fine boat!
Let's go for a ride!"

But GLUG!

GLUG!
GLUG!

The little boat sank...

...and the cat made a leap
and jumped back on the bank.

And what was he wearing,
that bad little cat?

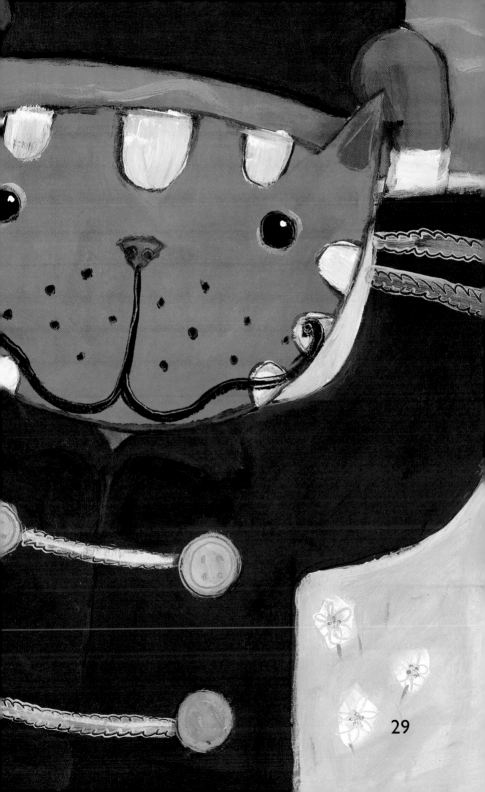

Oh yes! He was wearing a coat AND a hat!

Why not try reading another ZigZag book?

Dinosaur Planet ISBN 0 237 52793 6
by David Orme and Fabiano Fiorin

Tall Tilly ISBN 0 237 52794 4
by Jillian Powell and Tim Archbold

Batty Betty's Spells ISBN 0 237 52795 2
by Hilary Robinson and Belinda Worsley

The Thirsty Moose ISBN 0 237 52792 8
by David Orme and Mike Gordon

The Clumsy Cow ISBN 0 237 52790 1
by Julia Moffatt and Lisa Williams

Open Wide! ISBN 0 237 52791 X
by Julia Moffatt and Anni Axworthy

Too Small ISBN 0 237 52777 4
by Kay Woodward and Deborah van de Leijgraaf

I Wish I Was An Alien ISBN 0 237 52776 6
by Vivian French and Lisa Williams

The Disappearing Cheese ISBN 0 237 52775 8
by Paul Harrison and Ruth Rivers

Terry the Flying Turtle ISBN 0 237 52774 X
by Anna Wilson and Mike Gordon

Pet To School Day ISBN 0 237 52773 1
by Hilary Robinson and Tim Archbold

The Cat in the Coat ISBN 0 237 52772 3
by Vivian French and Alison Bartlett

32